The Guest at Red River

by

Cassi Elyse

Cover Illustrated by

Mason Harrison

Dedication:

For those who have always believed in me.

Special thanks to Mason, who supports and encourages me in so many ways, and who made me believe this was not only possible but a good idea, so much so that he graciously volunteered his own artwork to the cause.

And to Daniel. You keep me on my toes. As you grow up, I hope you always continue to indulge and expand your passion for reading and learning.

<u>PRESENT DAY</u>

He awoke in a sweat. He'd had the dream again.

It was always the same, the dream. He'd heard tell that some folks would dream in the abstract, fuzzy images, not really recalling details in the after. It wasn't so for him. He could retrace every shape and every motion start to end without even closing his eyes. At any given hour, he could picture that sailor's sunset in its brilliant splendor, as it gave way to the easy light of the harvest moon. Savoring each moment as if in a trance, he took pleasure in replaying the dream in his mind. The snap of a twig beneath his step, the scent of life seeping out from the pines and from every pore of his flesh. He knew each vivid detail as if he had lived it, as if it were a part of him. He felt every color…all shades of red.

It's the only dream he ever had. It was all he could remember, from what he could only presume was his former life. For purposes of this new life, he took to calling himself Mr. Rivers.

He couldn't say whether he'd been a bad man Before. He just knew, in his bones he knew, that he hadn't been a good man.

....

The Red River of the north is so named for the reddish brown silt it carries, an ancient relic of the long defunct Lake Agassiz. Some might say, though, that it's called Red because due to such calamities as battles and floodings and drownings and just plain bad men, it has seen more than its share of bloodshed. What stories it could tell… No matter the history behind its moniker, flowing north to Lake Winnipeg and eventually emptying into the Hudson Bay, the Red River lends its lifeblood to some of North America's most fertile farm country.

Mr. Fisher had found him in the creek on his property, off a tributary of the Red River. The creek had run aptly red that day, swelling up from a late spring rain, as red as Mr. Rivers imagined it had flowed the day he was born. Floating there amidst his newfound delirium, he was entranced by the face of his mother smiling down at him, an angel in white, her blonde locks flowing gently about her shoulders, as if she had joined him for a swim. Fisher had noticed him lying face up in the shallow water, a rotting tree trunk preventing him from drifting any further downstream. Fisher, agile and able for his age, entered the water and waded in toward the source of the ptomaine threatening his nostrils. Inhaling through his mouth didn't seem to help; somehow it made the stench even worse. Holding his breath instead, Fisher managed to haul the dead weight of the man to the water's edge, then – jumping back at the sound of a strangled cough escaping the lips of his supposed corpse – he grabbed at his back pocket for a rag which he instinctively held to the man's head wound. Only then did he notice it was still pulsing fresh red liquid. Fisher wasn't sure how this unfortunate stranger had any blood left in him, judging by the thick scarlet momentarily dammed up at the drowned log, full of death and stink. God knows what else had died in there.

Fisher glanced at the man's eyes, now open wide. For a moment, transfixed, Fisher noticed something in those dark pools that he recognized but couldn't quite label. The stranger's gaze seemed to drift up to Fisher's young daughter, waiting in youthful curiosity. She'd been splashing in the trough, her long yellow curls still drenched.

Fisher moved and the man looked back to him. Sharing a muted nod, Fisher managed to transform himself into both crutch and ambulance. Together they moved up the bank, then across the 50 yards or so to the humble farmhouse that Fisher and his family called home. No words were spoken. None were needed.

Fisher didn't think the man would survive, fading in and out of consciousness such as he was. As he finally blacked out, succumbing to the injuries for a while, he forgot about seeing his mother. He forgot everything.

....

He didn't know Fisher's actual name. Never asked, and Fisher returned the favor. Not that Rivers could have justified an answer anyway. None of the five residents of the farmhouse ever spoke, hardly, yet they seemed a content enough bunch, each with his or her own chores and lot to bear. Fisher and his family were kind to their injured stranger, compassionate even. Rivers didn't understand why, but it felt foreign to him. Uncomfortable. He wondered if he'd ever known comfort Before.

The two older children, a girl and a boy, had little to do with him. In the beginning, his recovery, they dutifully brought him his meals and tended to his bandages with a stolidity to rival that of the royal guards, but they always vanished as soon as the shift was through. He would see them through the window panes though, frolicking, even laughing at times. When their joy reached the audible like that, he would almost smile. It was a strange sensation on his face, and he was uncertain what to make of that.

The little one though, she brought with her an uneasiness that spread all over him like an itch.

He would study himself in the half-moon mirror there by his bed in the makeshift guestroom. It seemed more of a large closet – graced, much to his benefit, with a smallish window. He had a notion, based on the aptly muscled, sun hardened frame that glared back at him, that he must have been an intrepid entity in the Before, a formidable enemy had he been so inclined. But when she was near, the hairs on his arms and neck would prick up instantly. Too small yet to do any real harm, she was hardly an inimical presence but would enter his room most peaceably and watch him from the corner, some days for hours at a time. Just the two of them. Watching. Waiting, it seemed. For what, he knew not. That was their way from the start. Once Fisher had gotten him into the house and his wounds properly assessed, Rivers slept for two days straight, maybe more, only rousing slightly every few hours as Mother Fisher would gently force him awake for sips of water or warm broth. Even in his slumber, before he had ever seen or heard of the child, he was aware of her proximity. He just sensed it, felt the goosebumps in his very being, and he knew she was near.

After those first few days, healing was a restless endeavor in this provisional hospital ward. She would bring in her humble collection of toys and games, staring him down until he motioned for her to climb up with them. In the quiet still of the afternoons, they played, while Fisher was working and Mother schooling the two adolescents. He learned things on these quaint sunlit afternoons, with the fresh air streaming through the window, things he was most certain he'd never known Before – how to braid a doll's hair, sip daintily from the finest make-believe china teacups, draw purple ponies. True to form in this clan, she didn't say a word. Not one, not ever. Every so often though, her eyes would meet his for a long moment, then she would break into a grin so shiny he couldn't help but do the same. After the first few dozen encounters, it even started to feel natural. He still had the same feeling around her, but he could no longer call it uneasiness. It had become more…kindred. They were of the same essence. Perhaps it had thrown him off at first because, Before, it wasn't something he'd ever experienced. Of course, he couldn't know that for sure. He didn't like to think about what might have been Before anyway, except in the dream. So there they sat with their matching snaggletoothed grins, friends.

Eventually he convalesced enough so that Mother discharged him to work the fields with Fisher. There was a simple understanding among them that he had nowhere else to be. He steadily regained his strength, picked up quickly on the job duties, pulled his own weight. He and Fisher made a venerable and profitable team. There was no reason to consider moving on.

Some summer nights, the family and he would amble out the long dirt drive to where it branched off to a part of the river prime for swimming or fishing or chasing frogs. Rivers enjoyed seeing Fisher and Mother get the chance to have fun with the children. He didn't know what an Uncle felt like, but he liked to think he was sort of an uncle of the surrogate variety.

A couple years passed uneventful, until one summer evening a stranger arrived, disturbing the odd peace they had made as a family of six. Sharpening the kitchen knives, Rivers observed from a small work table in the corner as Fisher answered the door. The visitor claimed to be in the door-to-door sales business. Fisher let the man speak but kept him on the stoop, while the little one looked on from the opposite wall. Rivers watched as the visitor tried to sneak looks over Fisher's shoulder at the girl, his face taking the shape of a salesman's smile. Did some kids actually fall for that? He watched as she disappeared inside herself. Gripping her doll close, an unfamiliar expression cut sharply across her miniature features…one of silent panic melding before his very eyes with a piercing resolve. If not for her cheeks turning a hot crimson, no one else would have noticed the change in her. But Rivers did. He knew. He couldn't swear to it, but he thought he had seen that look once Before. He didn't like that color on her one bit.

The salesman rambled for another ten minutes before resigning himself to that fact that he wasn't going to be earning his day's pay at Fisher's place, so he got in his oversized two-tone brown Buick and sputtered away.

Lying in bed later that night, Rivers was disturbed in his spirit. Sleep came only in restless fits this night. The light of the full moon breaking through a row of pines at the edge of the property streamed a pale orange sliver through the thin curtains. He thought he saw movement in the bushes across the field. Deer, probably.

He dozed off momentarily, only to jolt upright in bed from the dream. The only dream.

Even summer nights were chilly in the north country, so he grabbed his lined jacket off the hook before starting for the door. Passing the little one's room, he noticed the curtains billowing slightly. It was peculiar for her window to be open at this hour. Warily, he peeked into the room. She wasn't in her bed. Rivers released himself from the doorway, entering the room completely, a certain feeling rising in him. Using his lighter to cut a path through the darkness, he stealthily checked the closet, then under the bed, ever vigilant not to disturb the other members of the family. Back outside her door, he peered down the darkened hallway. No light shone from the bathroom either.

He crept out the door and to the bottom of the four steps, before charging across the grass and out the driveway. His heart was racing before he even took off running. Instinctively, he headed straight for the river. He didn't know why, or what else he might find, but he knew she would be there and he knew that she must be protected.

The jaunt down the driveway seemed to take forever. Too long. As he finally approached the opening that led to the swimming hole, he thought he discerned a glint of metal just to the other side of the bushes. Breathless but trying not to make a sound, he checked in all directions. Best he could tell, he was alone. He edged deftly along the bushes, until at last he reached the entrance and slipped through unseen.

To his right, on the back side of bushes, his suspicion was confirmed, as the source of the metallic shine came into full view. It had come from an oversized two-tone brown Buick. He could see the bulk of the behemoth now that he rounded the corner, and there was no doubt in the conclusion he drew.

The salesman had never left.

Rivers made his way down the path, soft-stepping so as not to draw attention. It had been a rainy week, and out by the main road the river was raging loud, alive with current. He listened for other sounds. Beneath his worn brown boot, the snap of a twig. He slammed his eyes shut, trying to catch his already strained breath. He tried to engage other senses, keep himself grounded.

Honeysuckle and begonia and wet earth. Life. He could smell life dripping out from the trees and from the water and from himself. It was all very familiar. Too familiar? He didn't know, and certainly not in this context. He just knew that he needed to quell the panic. He needed to find her. To save her.

At last, he reached the sandy hill that they called the beach, and he stood at the shore. Turning his back to the water, he took in everything the eye could see by the full light of the moon, directly above him now and no longer encumbered.

Out of nowhere, something – someone? – rushed him and took them both into the water. Blindly kicking and punching for his life, he connected with human flesh, confirming both to his relief and chagrin that it wasn't an animal that had him. It was a worse kind of predator. Despite his initial injuries when Fisher had found him, he had long since recovered completely and – after years of helping on the farm since – was fit for a good fight. He was solid. Still, having been blindsided, he struggled to swim and fight simultaneously. Rivers managed to get the upper hand and finally landed a blow to the face that he now recognized as that of the salesman. They were close enough to the bank to try to get a foothold.

The salesman was more scrappy than he had appeared earlier, on the stoop slinging goods. He grappled beneath the surface until he got his hand on a heavy rock and, with a roundhouse swing, connected with the temple of the unfortunate Mr. Rivers. Momentarily advantaged by fazing his foe, the salesman was able to straddle his victim. Hoisting his newfound weapon in both hands, fully intent on crashing it down on his opponent's skull, the salesman abruptly became still, as a strange countenance crossed his face in the moonlight. Rivers could only stare in confusion as blood began to drizzle down the salesman's left cheek, and he fell off to the that side, the rock slipping from his hands and landing with a heavy splash as Rivers ducked away to avoid the impact.

Dazed but still in panic mode, Rivers scrambled to his knees in the shallows, hurling water from his lungs and trying desperately to replace it with heaving doses of air. Raising his head, he was taken by a vision: An angel in white, smiling down at him, blonde curls encasing her small face, round and delicate.

And it all came back to him.

....

<u>BEFORE</u>

You might say he had a type, this man we call Rivers. He could easily date it back to junior high school – maybe even younger, but in those formative early teenage years a pattern was undeniably taking up residence.

Mid-October was crisp in the Manitoban woods where he grew up, his father having fled to the region a draft dodger and a son of a bitch. He didn't remember much of his mother and had no stories of her to keep him warm at night. When she would cross his mind though, she felt like water, and so he felt closest to her there. He would catch a notion of a memory at the most random times – visions of swimming with her, chasing dragonflies along the riverbank together. He figured those were more a product of wishful imaginings, but he let himself dangle in them because tortured wishes were often more pleasant than his reality. And so it was that he was winding along the water's edge one frosty morning on his way to school, lost in his supposed recollections. The scent of snow hung imminent in the air. Almost to the school building, he cut through a thick row of jack pines and came upon the scene of a group of sophomores huddled up, laughing. He knew the boys by their letter jackets, and he could tell by their mocking sneers and the body language they imposed that they were fixing to dot the eyes of some kid of a no doubt lesser gene pool than they. From a great distance, he caught glimpses of a red hooded coat in the midst of the commotion, then the crowd of boys parted just right so that he could recognize the target of their affection as Jordan, the new kid.

Jordan was scrawny, a spectacled runt. Every letter jacket's dream.

Despite the stocky build and muscled limbs from logging with his father, he was not a fighter. Confrontation was not his nature. In fact, he made it his habit and his mission to go unnoticed, a skill he had picked up from years of trying to avoid his father's indiscriminate fits of temper. He had never been in a fight at school, never got in trouble of any kind, brought no attention on himself whatsoever. Stature be damned, he made himself small, unknowable. So it surprised even himself when instead of making a wide arc around the melee as he had done every single time before, he felt his steps guiding him closer to it until he was nearly nose to nose with the alpha bully. Mute, he made his presence known in other ways. He spoke not when spoken to, not a word when they ripped out clumps of his hair and called him every name in the book. Not a word when sucker punched. He doubled over momentarily then, but he was used to being kicked in the gut at home. Upright once more, he somehow stood taller than before. He was in truth a bit taller than most of the jocks, and twice as wide. Silently, motionless, he stared down the owner of the offending fist. No one would have been the wiser to the furnace of fury fulminating behind his deep blue eyes full of ice and calm. Alpha, possibly sensing he had blundered, snorted once, letting it linger in the air between them just for a moment before making tracks into the school building with his buddies.

Rivers took a few cautious breaths. His ribs ached. He knew the drill. Slowly, in and out, noting what caused pain and what didn't, so as to modify the process for the next couple days. He glanced around for Jordan, but the kid was smart. He must have bolted as soon as he realized a way out.

As the day wore on, he tried to focus on the lessons, but science and English and math all escaped him that day. He didn't seem to see the

board or the books, didn't hear the voices of the
teachers or his peers over the rush of blood
through his head. He just saw red. History class
almost had his attention for a moment with some
ancient bloody massacre, but it only touched off a
daydream in his addled mind.

Normally he did not look forward to going
home, but this day he couldn't get there fast
enough. When the final bell rang, he sprinted
straight to the wood shed and, despite the pain,
commenced to splitting and stacking firewood with
the determination of a mad man, wild eyes to
match. He didn't even notice when his father came
in, or the half-nod the man allowed in his
direction; it was the closest thing to approval or
affection the man ever offered. The boy was too
busy picturing Alpha and the gang finding
themselves on the business end of his trusty
hatchet. Over and over, he would hammer the butt
end of it down on their knees and hands, then bring
down the glistening blade, hacking off appendages,
slicing into bellies and chests and faces. He could
hear the crack of skulls rippling across the chilled
surface of the creek, could smell the blood as it
spurted from healthy young arteries and rushed
across the old plank floor of the lean-to and out the

door, still so fresh and warm it melted veins of red into the new powder outside. It created beautiful streaks of art on that empty white canvas. He could see it all so clearly that it felt almost real, certainly more real than anything else in his life. He lay awake in bed later wondering, Is this what it feels like to be alive?

He hardly slept that night, and when he did he dreamt of rivers flowing red with blood, yet he rose early. He sat on the edge of the bed a while, contemplating his existence. His reflection stared back from the cracked, dirty bathroom mirror for a long time. Did he really look like that? Was he cracked and dirty too? Leaning in closer, he tried to see what there might be behind his eyes. A soul? A human? A few more years, and he would be grown. Would he be a good man, or would he be a bad man? On his visage were the makings of something most certainly, but some thing that he wouldn't understand until much later.

He arrived at school early that morning in spite of his bruised belly and shoulder blades afire. He caught sight of a red hooded jacket entering the door, a group of jocks loitering at the foot of the steps. To his great pleasure, the latter collective all gave a start when they saw him striding toward those same steps. They jumped and scattered, dropping pencils and books, Alpha's Poe essay blowing away on the wind only to land and shrivel in a mud puddle. Couple degrees colder and it would've been frozen over but, as it was, the paper was ruined. Had he ever heard of karma, he might've believed in it for that moment.

He ambled up the stairs, down the hall, and had quietly settled into his seat in the back when he noticed Jordan two chairs over in the next row up. Jordan had watched him enter and gave a crooked grin upon recognition; it looked as though he might have waved too but then thought better of it. Unsure how to react to a kindness, however simple as a smile, he simply raised his chin in acknowledgement before turning his attention to his raggedy book bag. As the rest of the class filed in, the jocks took their usual places in the front rows. He couldn't help noticing that they were unusually quiet, their faces shielded from his line of sight. The history book on his desk had fallen open to a page on war, some tragic battle from who cares what century. Looking down at the script though, he smiled to himself. It was an odd sensation on his face. Letting his gaze fall back over Jordan for a second, then settle on the instigators, he felt for the first time like he might have a place in the world. He began to see himself as a guardian angel of sorts, defender of the meek. He could've been a bully to the bullies but, in honing his newfound craft, he found that more often than not he need only look the ringleader in the eye and the whole bunch ran away, tails tucked neatly between their legs. They acted tough, but they were feeble and useless. They made him angry, with their taunts and their tricks, picking on the little guys, the outcasts. But mostly it was their inflated sense of self. They knew they couldn't back up their threats, and now he knew it too. They were posers, imposters, just jackasses playing pretend, hiding behind their pathetic high school fame, little brats shielding themselves with mommy's apron. He couldn't stand it. They made him very angry. And, he found, he liked being angry.

And thus, his type was formed, at so tender and impressionable an age. He began to fantasize it constantly, slicing and dicing them, bashing in their heads, bleeding them dry. He paid special attention in biology class, mapping out in his mind the locations of all the big arteries, committing them to memory. His art projects varied, keeping in theme with the assignments, so the instructor never noticed that they consisted solely of the colors of blood and flesh, steel and wood. He stalked those letter jackets incessantly, class to class, always unnoticed, moving on autopilot, daydreaming all the way, so evenings and weekends he had a decent storehouse pent up and found boundless satisfaction taking axe to logs for hours on end. He wondered if he would become a serial killer. He killed people all the time in his daydreams, bad people.

....

Time went by. His seventeenth birthday was approaching. The letter jackets had aged out, and the next generation of them arrived, but these seemed to have inherited the knowledge that he was untouchable and so, by extension, were the little guys. He didn't miss the drama. Didn't need it to get his fix, for it was always there, at the forefront of his mind. He could look at them and tell they were bad, and that's all it took. Go to school. Get angry. Come home. Chop things. Feel better.

His wrath was not reserved for just his peers at school. He had started making the food and beer runs after his father's foot got mangled in a bear trap and he had to stay off it for six weeks. The boy would get good and angry on those runs too. He could tell bad men from good ones. He just knew.

And bad men were everywhere.

A month into it, he had been on one of these excursions and was nearly home with an armful of PBR for his father. Behind the creek and the woods on the other side of the modest hut that they called home, the sun was just beginning its descent to the horizon, setting the scene ablaze with implications of its oranges and pinks. Almost to the wood shed, he watched the old man hobble across the porch toward a stray black Labrador, her clearly pregnant belly distorted and offset against a lifetime of hunger. Leaning his full weight on his crutch, deliberately and without threat of remorse, the old man reared back his good leg and with all his might aimed his steel toe directly into the lab's swaying belly.

The bag of brew slipped from the boy's hands and fell to the ground as he looked on in horror, the distance between them close enough so that he had a clear view yet still too far to try to stop it from happening. He heard the glass bottles hit the ground and thunk one against another, at least one of them shattering and sending the liquid foam spraying up through the air and all over his face and hair as he bent down to reach for them. When he did so, the mahogany handle of his axe hanging in the shed caught his eye. Standing, he snapped to attention, jaw set, eyes narrowed. His breath flowed slow and even, displaying a calm in contrast to the implosion of rage within. He stepped over the beer bottles and in two quick strides grabbed his hatchet, his only friend in the world and the one who knew all his secrets. Seeing his reflection in the window of the shed, he could now comprehend the expression that had glared back at him so long ago from the dirty, cracked mirror.

The old man had knocked himself off balance with the momentum of his kick, and he lay there on the steps, laughing at the injured animal as she yelped, weeping for her unborn pups. The bastard was laughing. The boy had never heard his father so much as chuckle before, and hurting an innocent animal was the ticket? The shadow he cast over his father that day as he silently raised his blade high above his head, hair and face still dripping with the bittersweet liquid, said more about their relationship than words ever had.

The old man never had to worry about staying off that foot again. He didn't laugh anymore either.

....

His brain grappled to come back to the present as Mr. Rivers. Once again lying in the water, the sins of the day floating downstream never to be heard from again, he found himself gazing on that uniquely familiar expression in the face of this small child, except now those golden curls that ringed her cheeks were damp with the unmistakable rosy tint of manslaughter. The salesman lay crumpled to the side, half in the water, half on the bank, an axe driven deep into his cranium.

Rivers looked at the little one. She wasn't happy at what had just transpired. But she wasn't sad over it either. She simply understood that she did what had to be done. And so, finally, did he.

She wasn't the one who had needed saving. While he may never recall how he ended up in the Red River the first time, there was no doubt that it took him to where he belonged, to where he fit in this world.